SOULFUL SYDNEY EXPLORES DIVERSITY

Written by: Mariam Azeez, Terry Murphy & Deborah Clarke
Illustrated by: Tian

Copyright 2018 Deborah Clarke

ISBN: 978-0-692-10445-3
(Also available for Kindle)

Published by Soulful Sydney Press

Sydney and her dog Max see new neighbors next door
And Sydney tells Max, "I hope there are kids like before."

Wondering together who they might be,
They count parents and a girl—a family of three.

Eagerly, Sydney runs on ahead
Cautiously, Max takes a bit longer to tread;

For covering the girl's head is a scarf of dark blue
And Max is suspicious of anything new.

He started to growl, fear raising his hair,
Baring his teeth through a menacing glare.

Beneath the blue scarf were chocolate brown eyes
And a smile so sweet it would be hard to disguise
The warmth and the kindness when her friendly voice called
To Sydney who became completely enthralled.

She said, "My name is Sydney and my dog who seems rude
Is Max whose fear sometimes ruins his mood."

Nodding, the girl said,
"A hijab can seem like something strange
But talking about it helps people—and dogs!—to change."

Petting Max to soothe him,
Sydney said, "Help me understand!"
And the girl with the big eyes held out a friendly hand.
"My name is Mariam and if you come beside me to sit
I'll share my lunch and tell you all about it."

"Thank you so much," replied Sydney, feeling happy,
And even Max stopped acting mean and snappy.
While Mariam explained the hijab upon her head,
They took time to relax and together break bread.

As they sat under the shade of a giant oak tree,
Becoming good friends, this party of three,
Mariam said, "Muslims aren't about hocus pocus;
Character, dignity, and respect are our main focus.
I wish there was a place where we could all learn
About religions and cultures and all kids get a turn."

Sydney exclaimed, "Maybe if we look, we'll find such a place
Where there's regard for all faiths and respect for each race."

And so Sydney asked Mariam to join on a quest
To put their theory of acceptance to the test.
Through the garden gate, the answers were near;
Little did they know, it was crystal clear
That by adopting just the right attitude,
They could enter into the Garden of Gratitude!

GRATITUDE
GARDEN

Counting their blessings as the gate opened wide,
Sydney and Mariam became each other's guide.
They found the entrance by being grateful and kind
On this journey to a place to quiet their minds.

GRATITUDE
GARDEN

With awe and respect, through the Garden they wander
Until they find a pond where they can ponder
About the world they want to create,
A world of understanding, not of hate.

At this Pondering Pond, they see their reflection
That's free of prejudice, hostility, and rejection.

At the Field of Forgiveness, they pause to assess
What has made this world such an unpleasant mess.
It's there that they realize in order to live
People must be willing to overcome and forgive

And come to an agreement that this world is a place
To fill with compassion, kindness, and grace.

Arm in arm, as they travel to their destination
They realize the value of how education
Will help them to spread harmony and peace
And convince all people that hatred must cease.

They avoided Camp Chaos at Belly Acres Farm
Where everyone seems to be constantly alarmed!

Under a Tranquil Tree, they sat and got quiet
Even Max settled down and decided to try it!

Serene and calm in a meditative pose,
Both girls relaxed with their eyes gently closed.
This moment of silence was all they would need
For the girls to accept that they must proceed.

They would soon understand as they continued their tour
They would find the remedy that would help to cure
So many of the ills that affect humankind
With education and respect and an open mind.

Rounding a corner, such a sight they did see—
Children sharing and playing and laughing with glee.
Kids of all faiths and colors of skin
Yet treating each other like they were kin.

Diversity University was the destination
Where Sydney and Mariam stared in fascination--
They saw Christians and Muslims and Jewish kids, too
Buddhists and Taoists as well as Hindu.

Catholics and Protestants and Baha'i—
There was no way that anyone could deny
That peace and harmony had been found
With acceptance and kindness all around.

This place is not depicted on any map or chart
It ultimately resides inside each person's heart.

Your own compassion can always be found
If you keep your mind open and just look around.

Be grateful for the differences as we learn to accept
Why it's more vital to include than it is to reject
People whose background is different from yours
And whose story and beliefs you should explore.
For when people find love in a world of hate
Loving kindness is the language they create.

My name is Mariam and I'm 11 years old. I am an American Muslim that follows and practices the faith of Islam. The Arabic word "Islam" is based on the root "salama," which means peace or surrender to God. Muslims who follow the right teachings of Islam are peaceful and loving people. When we greet people, we say "Assalamu Alaikum" which means, "Peace be upon you." Islam is a monotheistic faith. We believe in The One God and Muhammad (Peace Be Upon Him) is a Prophet of God. We pray 5 times a day, give charity to the poor and needy, and fast during the month of Ramadan. We make a pilgrimage to Mecca at least once in a lifetime, if we are mentally, physically, and financially able to do so. By practicing these beliefs, we strive to be kind, patient, and good human beings, to ourselves and to the world around us. Muslims celebrate two main holidays, Eid-Ul-Fitr and Eid-Ul-Adha.

Eid ul-Fitr is a celebration that marks the end of Ramadan, the holy month of fasting where we fast from sunrise to sunset. Fasting teaches us to be patient and feel with the people who are less fortunate than us. I like it because it's time for us to reflect on ourselves and know our weaknesses in our character so that we may strengthen them. Spending the night at the mosque for the night prayer in Ramadan (Taraweeh) gives me a chance to see my friends everyday.

Eid-Ul-Adha is known as the Feast of Sacrifice or " The Greater Eid". The festival remembers Prophet Ibrahim's (Abraham's) willingness to sacrifice his son when God ordered him to. At this festival, we sacrifice a sheep as a reminder of Ibrahim's obedience to God. We share the meat with our families, friends, and the poor people of the community. Both Eids usually start with us going to the Mosque for prayers, dressed in our best traditional clothes, thanking Allah (God) for all the blessings we have received.

On the following pages, I have invited other children of different faiths to share their beliefs and traditions.

May peace be upon them and YOU!

"I am a Catholic."
Spencer
Age- 6

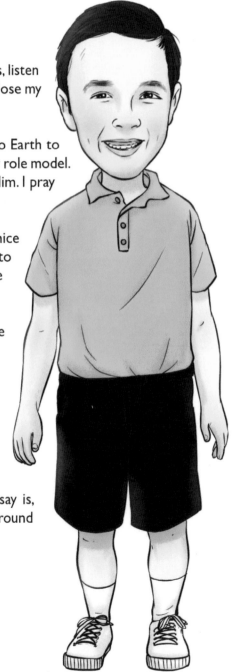

I go to a Catholic church every Sunday with my family to sing songs, listen to Bible stories and thank God for my blessings with my prayers. I close my eyes and make sure that I am focusing and listening to God.

Jesus lived a very long time ago. Jesus is God's Son who He sent to Earth to be a good example for all of us. He is special to me because he is my role model. God is very important to me because I would not exist without Him. I pray to Him every night.

I enjoy hearing Bible stories about Jesus to understand ways to be nice and kind to others and treat others the way I would want them to treat me. It is important to be a good Catholic person and care about everyone and nature.

The Pope and priests are leaders of the church who follow all of the nice things Jesus did.

I was Baptized when I was a baby, and soon I will have First Communion. Baptism and Communion are called Sacraments. I like celebrating Easter and Christmas with my family because Christmas is when Jesus was born and Easter is when Jesus went up to Heaven to be with God.

Every night I pray before I go to sleep, and the last thing that I say is, "Jesus, let me walk in your light and let me be a light to others around me."

"I am a Lutheran"
Daniel
Age- 9

Every Sunday I go to Our Saviour Lutheran Church with my family. Some Sundays I am an acolyte and I really enjoy that. I think about God when I'm an acolyte.

When I'm an acolyte I get dressed in a robe and I walk down the aisle at the beginning of church behind the cross, with my candlelighter. I get to light the two candles at the front of the church and then I sit at the front and listen to the service. At the end of church I get to put the candles out with the bell snuffer and walk back down the aisle.

I was asked to be an acolyte ever since I made my first holy communion. I took classes with our pastor and learned a lot about God and the last supper. I get to eat a wafer and have wine.

I enjoy going to church. When I'm an acolyte it is my favorite because it keeps me busy and involved in the service.

"What it's Like to be Jewish"
Matthew
Age- 12

I've learned so much in my years being a Jew. One thing I've learned is that being a Jew is hard. All Jews need to do a lot of hard work and training for a big ceremony that happens when you're twelve or thirteen years old. These ceremonies are called either a "bar mitzvah" if you're a boy, or a "bat mitzvah" if you're a girl. These ceremonies consist of a two- to three-hour-long service, depending on what type of Judaism you follow, and then later, a huge party! During this party, there will be dancing, games, delicious food, and your candle lighting. So when you think about it, your years worth of training pays off in the end. Another thing I've learned about being Jewish is that it's so much fun! There are so many fun Jewish holidays! Some of the most important include Hanukkah, Purim, Passover, Rosh Hashanah, and Yom Kippur. I love Hanukkah because it's a time to see family, receive presents, and most importantly, eat latkes. Latkes are a delicious fried potato pancake that Jews eat during Hanukkah. Another holiday is Rosh Hashanah, which is the New Year for the Jews.

"I am a Baha'i"
Clovy
Age- 9

One of the things that I like about my Faith is that we have a whole prayer book of our Writings to read from. You are actually saying the Prophet's Writings so we do not have to make up our own prayers.

I like that my Faith teaches that everyone is one family and the world is one home. My Faith teaches that we should be kind no matter what anyone does to us. I have never met a Baha'i who was not kind to me.

I also like in my Faith that we have many holidays. It feels special to celebrate when no one else is celebrating. Each holiday has a story that we can share when we gather together.

I love my Faith because it teaches we should have peace and unity all over the world. And you can tell when you look at our Faith because it is extremely diverse.

"I respect Taoism but I am not a Taoist"
Brisamina
Age- 12

I am not a Taoist. I just loosely follow what I have been taught is a form of Taoism.

Being a 'Taoist' to me is really just respecting others and their ways of life.

I myself do not necessarily believe there is a god, or even many gods, however, I do believe that every story has a grain of truth.

I believe there were humans so great they were labeled gods. For example, while I do not believe that the Greek goddess Hera was in fact a goddess, I do believe there may have been an influential woman who was labeled as such for her great acts.

As such, since I have no real 'practices' I try to do things that energize me, I try to do things that I love doing, things that will be enjoyable to do. Some of these things include reading, I typically read 3-4 hours a day, I also enjoy drawing and painting. This helps me to relax and get through the things that I don't enjoy as much.

Self portrait by Brisamina

"Hindu"
Esha
Age- 9

My mom is from a Hindu family and my dad is from a Catholic family. My understanding of Hinduism is that it has many gods which stand for different things like knowledge, protecting people. I know of a few... Lord Rama, Hanuman, Lord Krishna and Ganpati. Many are forms of three main gods which come to earth in human or animal form to help people. In Hinduism, these have always been called avatars. We have two little statues in my home and my grandparents like many Hindus have a little temple at home. I also like the peaceful practice of yoga, which started from Hinduism. It helps me with gymnastics.

My favorite festival is Diwali. It celebrates Lord Rama's return from 14 years of war and a win over evil Ravana. During this time, in my house I light diyas, which are clay lanterns and draw colorful rangoli on our front porch. It is a festival of lots of lights and happiness to celebrate good over evil. We make Diwali sweets at home. It is a lot of fun to light fireworks ! We also do bhau beez during Diwali, which celebrates brother sister bond (I have an older brother, do a small pooja and I get a gift!).

"Zen Buddhist"
Miles
Age- 6

I like being Zen Buddhist because it's calm. I like meditating. I think it's right to not kill animals to get meat.

The first time I went to the Zen monastery was Buddha's birthday weekend celebration. I liked it so much, I asked my Mom if we could move to the monastery! I like the shape of the buildings. It's like Ninjago. We go there during my school vacations sometimes. There is a Dharma School for kids. We run around the woods and play in the Peace Pagoda, too. One cool and kind of funny thing about Buddha is his hairstyle.

The chanting at the Zen Center is my favorite. I like the sound of the bell in the morning. Sometimes there are retreats and everybody sings and meditates together. It's nice to go there with my Mom. It's fun.

Terry Murphy is the creator and storyteller of the Soulful Sydney series. Her zeal for creating a world of justice, inclusion, and love for her own grandchildren is the driving force behind her desire to make the world a better place for ALL children.

Mariam Azeez is the eleven-year-old originator of the storyline as well as the archetype for the delightful Muslim character who introduces Sydney to a broader horizon.

Deborah Clarke is the poet and editor for this project who, like her sister, is a grandmother seeking to awaken a sense of unity and acceptance in future generations.

A special thank you goes to **Christina Connors** who is the co-creator of the original concept. She is also a talented singer and performer. ChristinaConnors.com

Illustrated by the very talented **Tian** whose inspired vision created magic.

Follow Soulful Sydney on Facebook and Twitter @SoulfulKidSyd

Made in the USA
Columbia, SC
04 June 2018